## THE MEXICAN NATION

On September 16, 1810, Miguel Hidalgo, a priest born in New Spain, proclaimed Mexico's independence. This day, celebrated as *Día de la Independencia*, began a struggle that lasted until 1821, when Mexico finally broke free of Spain. Then, for more than 100 years, Mexico faced many troubles, including civil war, war with the United States, and finally a revolution to bring social and economic changes. The Mexican flag represents the rich history of this country and the long road toward becoming a modern democracy. The coat of arms refers to a legend that the Aztecs built their capital city where they saw an eagle standing on a cactus with a snake in its beak. The green of the flag stands for independence, the white for religious belief, and the red for union. Proud Mexican citizens today can stroll the streets of Mexico City and see Aztec temples, Spanish churches, and modern skyscrapers — all part of Mexico's heritage. *Viva México!*

## CHAPULTEPEC PARK

Pequeña's park has seen all the long history of Mexico City. The Aztecs settled there before the year 1300, and the name of the park is Aztec for "grasshopper hill." Montezuma's collection of animals at Chapultepec may have been the world's first zoo. In colonial times, Chapultepec became a public park, and a castle was built there which housed European rulers and Mexican presidents. The park was later the scene of a famous battle during the war between Mexico and the United States. Today Chapultepec Park is the perfect place for a holiday picnic or a special birthday party.

# Pequeña the Burro

Written by **Jami Parkison**

Illustrated by **Itoko Maeno**

MarshMedia, Kansas City, Missouri

*Dedicated to Mama,*
*as all things eventually are.*

*Special thanks to John Parkison, Jane Mobley,*
*John Dixon, and Sandy Beaty.*

Text © 1994 by Marsh Film Enterprises, Inc.
Illustrations © 1994 by Itoko Maeno

First Printing 1994
Second Printing 1999
Third Printing 2003

Published by **MARSH**media

    A Division of Marsh Film Enterprises, Inc.
    P. O. Box 8082
    Shawnee Mission, KS 66208

**Library of Congress Cataloging-in-Publication Data**
Parkison, Jami.
   Pequeña the burro/written by Jami Parkison; illustrated by Itoko Maeno.
     p.  cm.
   Summary: Despite her feeling that she is only a burro, Pequeña is
able to live up to the noble heritage of her ancestors who helped
build Mexico.
    ISBN 1-55942-055-3
   [1. Donkeys—Fiction.  2. Self-confidence—Fiction.
3. Mexico—Fiction.]  I. Maeno, Itoko, ill.  II. Title.
PZ7.P2394Pe 1994                      93-30377
[E]—dc20      Z0063365 5-06

*Book layout and typography by Cirrus Design*

Printed in China

Every weekend Pequeña's park became a carnival of delights. Families gathered for picnics and celebrations. Merchants traded their colorful wares. Kites danced across the sky. Chapultepec Park had everything — a zoo, lakes, theaters, gardens, a miniature railroad, a bullring — even a castle.

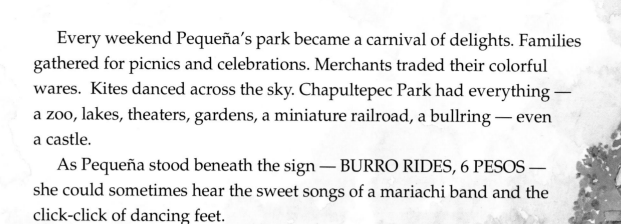

As Pequeña stood beneath the sign — BURRO RIDES, 6 PESOS — she could sometimes hear the sweet songs of a mariachi band and the click-click of dancing feet.

On weekends, children lined up for a chance to ride the burros. *"Ándale, ándale!"* they squealed, as Pequeña carried them around the corral.

But on this particular weekend, something very special had happened.

Pequeña had been invited to a birthday party.

Pequeña was eating breakfast when the girl and her mother stopped by the corral. "I want the tiny, gray one, *por favor,*" the girl said and patted Pequeña's soft muzzle. That's how Pequeña was chosen.

She had never gone to a party before.

"I'd hate to be in your shoes," Bonita said after the little girl left. Although a circus clown once owned Bonita, she was the gloomiest burro Pequeña had ever met. Sabio, the oldest burro in the corral, said that Bonita could find a storm cloud in the sunniest sky.

Bonita shook her head gravely. "Do you realize that little girl is the daughter of Captain Alvarez, the great charro rider?"

"Charro rider?" Pequeña asked.

"A great horseman, *sí*. Poor Pequeña. He'll watch you like a hawk. Be careful," Bonita warned. "Tons of things can go wrong at a party. If a balloon pops and frightens you, you might drop one of the children, or in the hot sun, you could get tired and faint. Tons and tons —"

"Oh, be quiet, Bonita," Pequeña said. "Nothing will go wrong." But in spite of Pequeña's brave words, Bonita had planted the seeds of doubt.

That morning Pequeña made her way through the park carrying baskets of flowers for the vendor who had rented her for the day.

Passing the zoo, Pequeña watched the elephants. "If I had the broad back of an elephant," she thought, "I would never drop a rider."

When she passed the lion cages, Pequeña heard the roar of the king of beasts. "If I had the power of the big cats," Pequeña thought, "I wouldn't jump at a silly balloon."

Pequeña passed the long-necked swans. "If I were a swan gliding across a cool lake," Pequeña thought, "I wouldn't faint under the heat of the sun."

Later, returning to the corral, Pequeña saw a crowd gathered near the bridle paths. Sleek horses clipped along the path. Proud riders sat ramrod straight in their saddles. They wore tight pants and short jackets. Their spurs jingled and their sombreros bounced in rhythm with the canter.

These were the famous Mexican charro riders, practicing for next week's parade marking *Día de la Independencia* — the day in 1810 when Father Miguel Hidalgo declared Mexico's independence from Spain.

Pequeña had never seen anything so glorious as the charro riders and their high-stepping horses.

Right then, Pequeña saw a strange reflection in a window.

At first she didn't
know who that animal was. A
squat thing with coarse fur, it
looked like a cartoon horse,
something created to make
people laugh.

And then Pequeña
recognized the baskets.
It was Pequeña's reflection
in the glass!

Pequeña had never felt so miserable. Useless as a broken toy. Common as a washrag. Fancy ribbons would never transform her into something special enough for a birthday party.

"Why the long face?" Sabio asked when Pequeña trudged into the corral at siesta time.

"I'm a burro," Pequeña said.

"Of course, you're a burro," Sabio said.

"I mean, I'm *only* a burro."

Sabio's face darkened.

"Listen to me, Pequeña," Sabio said. "There's no such thing as *only* a burro. Who do you think helped build all this — this city, this country? Ever since the first burro set foot on this land — 500 years ago — we have labored to build Mexico. We transported settlers into a new world, we hauled bricks, we pulled plows, we brought water to desert cities."

"So much work —" Pequeña began.

"We hauled gold and silver down steep mountain trails."

"Gold and silver?" Pequeña asked in wonder.

"*Sí*. Sometimes our shoes were forged from gold or silver. We carried so much rich ore that those metals were more plentiful than iron. Your ancestors, Pequeña, wore silver and gold shoes."

"I didn't know, Sabio."

Sabio yawned. "There's a lot you don't know, Pequeña. Songs have been written about us, statues created to commemorate our contributions, cities named in our honor. Pequeña, you share the proud heritage of all Mexico." And then he added, in a sleepy whisper, "There's no such thing, Pequeña, as only a burro."

Early Sunday morning, Pequeña was dressed for the party. The corral owner tied satin bows in her mane and braided ribbons through her tail. He hooked a dainty yellow cart to her shoulder harness.

At the party, the children swarmed around her. "Me first!" they shouted. The Alvarez family had roped off a wooded section of the park with streamers. Balloons floated in the trees. Near a huge, concrete picnic table dangled an *estrella*, the classic star-shaped *piñata*.

On the table was a feast. Pequeña had never seen so much food: cakes, platters of tacos, mounds of fajitas, and pitchers of lemonade.

All morning, the children rode Pequeña. The littlest ones rode in the cart, while many of the older children rode on Pequeña's back.

When a balloon broke loose and snagged on a limb, Pequeña remembered Bonita's gloomy warnings. But by then it was lunch time, and the children were feeding Pequeña carrots and apples. It was easy to forget gloomy warnings.

After lunch everyone gathered
under the *piñata*. Maria Alvarez was
blindfolded. Using a wooden pole, she
batted at the star.

"Higher, Maria!" someone called.
Maria nicked the red point of the star.

"To the left!"

Maria flattened the bright blue
point of the star.

"Down a little!"

With one fierce blow, Maria
smashed the *piñata's* center.

Candy and small toys rained down on the children, who scrambled over the grass and bounded across the picnic table, gathering up prizes.

Just then . . . CRACK . . . . the table began to collapse. Crumbling concrete sounded like thunder. Finally, the broken slabs settled precariously against the pedestal.

At that moment, a tiny voice called out, "Mama. Papa."

It was Maria Alvarez. She was caught inside the rubble.

"Don't touch it," someone warned. "The whole thing may cave in."

"If we could move this big piece —" someone began.

"It's too heavy."

Pequeña picked up one end of the cart rope. She walked to the concrete debris and dropped the rope.

"The burro. We'll use the burro," said Captain Alvarez.

Pequeña backed up to the broken table. Two people eased a loop of rope around the biggest piece. Señora Alvarez tied the ends to the harness.

Pequeña slowly pressed her weight forward until the rope was taut. She could feel the muscles in her neck swell against the tremendous resistance of the concrete.

"Steady," Captain Alvarez guided Pequeña.

Pequeña strained until her shoulder muscles burned, her legs ached. But no matter how hard she struggled, the concrete wouldn't budge.

A crowd soon gathered. News of the accident had spread throughout the park. For the first time, Pequeña wavered. All eyes were upon her, all hopes pinned on a little burro. "What have I gotten myself into?" she wondered.

And then, from somewhere in the crowd, Pequeña thought she heard a familiar voice. "There is no such thing as only a burro."

"Just a little more —" Señora Alvarez called.

Pequeña pressed on. The heat from the sun and the heat from the effort were nearly suffocating.

And then Pequeña felt the rope suddenly go slack.

There was a loud crash, and Pequeña pitched forward on her knees.
"*Olé!*" the crowd roared.
Pequeña looked around as Captain and Señora Alvarez lifted Maria from the wreckage.

The Alvarezes set Maria beside Pequeña. *"Mi amiga,"* Maria said, hugging the burro's neck.

Señora Alvarez stroked Pequeña's damp fur. *"Gracias."*

"This deserves more than thanks," Captain Alvarez said.

And so, on the day of Mexico's most patriotic fiesta, Pequeña was there. The little burro marched in the *Día de la Independencia* parade. And what's more, she led the magnificent column of charro riders and Captain Alvarez.

All along the boulevards of Mexico City, the people shouted with joy at seeing the burro who saved the little girl.

"Viva Pequeña . . .
Viva el burro . . .
Viva México!"

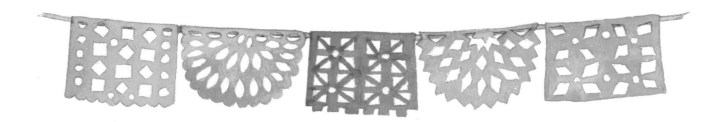

Dear Parents and Educators:

All Americans are immigrants or descendants of immigrants. Beginning with the first nomadic hunter-gatherers who crossed the ice-packed bridge from Asia to Alaska tens of thousands of years ago, we all have roots elsewhere. To define our heritage is no simple matter.

In modern-day Mexico, small banners of intricately-cut paper, called *papel picado*, flutter over rural markets, across urban windows and balconies, from the ceilings of Catholic churches. One authority on Mexican arts and crafts explains that the making of *papel picado* came to America from Spain, along with the Chinese rice paper used to create them. But to understand the enduring meaning and popularity of these lacy works of art, we must look back to the revered status of paper in pre-Columbian times and its use in religious rituals. The paper of China, the craft of Spain, and the spirit world of ancient Mexico are joined in these festive decorations of today.

There are many reasons for young people in the United States to learn about Mexico's rich cultural heritage. On a practical level, our neighbor to the south is vitally important to our own country's economic and political well-being. Also, Mexican-Americans are one of the fastest-growing political forces in the United States. But most important, when children learn about their own or another's heritage, they learn more about their individual identities and about the cultural threads that tie all people together. Like Pequeña, they discover the strengths that lie in diversity as well as in unity.

Here are some questions you might ask to help children think about the message of **Pequeña the Burro:**

- At the beginning of the story, what special event was Pequeña looking forward to?

- How did gloomy Bonita plant the seeds of doubt in Pequeña's mind?

- What did Pequeña think when she compared herself to the elephants? To the lions? To the swans? To the charro horses?

- What did Sabio tell Pequeña about her heritage?

- Our heritage includes many things, such as language, religion, traditions, and family history. What are some things you know about your heritage?

- How is your heritage different from the heritage of someone you know? How is it the same?

Here are some ways you can help children value their own and others' heritages:

- Explore the history and meaning of family and community traditions.

- Take advantage of opportunities to learn about and participate in the celebrations and traditions of others.

- Recognize special contributions children are able to make because of their unique heritages.

# *Available from MarshMedia*

These storybooks, each hardcover with dustjacket and full-color illustrations throughout, are available at bookstores, or you may order by calling MarshMedia toll free at 1-800-821-3303.

*Amazing Mallika*, written by Jami Parkison, illustrated by Itoko Maeno. 32 pages. ISBN 1-55942-087-1.

*Bailey's Birthday*, written by Elizabeth Happy, illustrated by Andra Chase. 32 pages. ISBN 1-55942-059-6.

*Bastet*, written by Linda Talley, illustrated by Itoko Maeno. 32 pages. ISBN 1-55942-161-4.

*Bea's Own Good*, written by Linda Talley, illustrated by Andra Chase. 32 pages. ISBN 1-55942-092-8.

*Clarissa*, written by Carol Talley, illustrated by Itoko Maeno. 32 pages. ISBN 1-55942-014-6.

*Dream Catchers*, written by Lisa Suhay, illustrated by Louis S. Glanzman. 40 pages. ISBN 1-55942-181-9.

*Emily Breaks Free*, written by Linda Talley, illustrated by Andra Chase. 32 pages. ISBN 1-55942-155-X.

*Feathers at Las Flores*, written by Linda Talley, illustrated by Andra Chase. 32 pages. ISBN 1-55942-162-2.

*Following Isabella*, written by Linda Talley, illustrated by Andra Chase. 32 pages. ISBN 1-55942-163-0.

*Gumbo Goes Downtown*, written by Carol Talley, illustrated by Itoko Maeno. 32 pages. ISBN 1-55942-042-1.

*Hana's Year*, written by Carol Talley, illustrated by Itoko Maeno. 32 pages. ISBN 1-55942-034-0.

*Inger's Promise*, written by Jami Parkison, illustrated by Andra Chase. 32 pages. ISBN 1-55942-080-4.

*Jackson's Plan*, written by Linda Talley, illustrated by Andra Chase. 32 pages. ISBN 1-55942-104-5.

*Jomo and Mata*, written by Alyssa Chase, illustrated by Andra Chase. 32 pages. ISBN 1-55942-051-0.

*Kiki and the Cuckoo*, written by Elizabeth Happy, illustrated by Andra Chase. 32 pages. ISBN 1-55942-038-3.

*Kylie's Concert*, written by Patty Sheehan, illustrated by Itoko Maeno. 32 pages. ISBN 1-55942-046-4.

*Kylie's Song*, written by Patty Sheehan, illustrated by Itoko Maeno. 32 pages. (Advocacy Press) ISBN 0-911655-19-0.

*Ludmila's Way*, written by Linda Talley, illustrated by Andra Chase. 32 pages. ISBN 1-55942-190-8.

*Minou*, written by Mindy Bingham, illustrated by Itoko Maeno. 64 pages. (Advocacy Press) ISBN 0-911655-36-0.

*Molly's Magic*, written by Penelope Colville Paine, illustrated by Itoko Maeno. 32 pages. ISBN 1-55942-068-5.

*My Way Sally*, written by Mindy Bingham and Penelope Paine, illustrated by Itoko Maeno. 48 pages. (Advocacy Press) ISBN 0-911655-27-1.

*Papa Piccolo*, written by Carol Talley, illustrated by Itoko Maeno. 32 pages. ISBN 1-55942-028-6.

*Pequeña the Burro*, written by Jami Parkison, illustrated by Itoko Maeno. 32 pages. ISBN 1-55942-055-3.

*Plato's Journey*, written by Linda Talley, illustrated by Itoko Maeno. 32 pages. ISBN 1-55942-100-2.

*Tessa on Her Own*, written by Alyssa Chase, illustrated by Itoko Maeno. 32 pages. ISBN 1-55942-064-2.

*Thank You, Meiling*, written by Linda Talley, illustrated by Itoko Maeno, 32 pages. ISBN 1-55942-118-5.

*Time for Horatio*, written by Penelope Paine, illustrated by Itoko Maeno. 48 pages. (Paper Posie, LLC) ISBN 0-9707944-7-9.

*Toad in Town*, written by Linda Talley, illustrated by Itoko Maeno. 32 pages. ISBN 1-55942-165-7.

*Tonia the Tree*, written by Sandy Stryker, illustrated by Itoko Maeno. 32 pages. (Advocacy Press) ISBN 0-911655-16-6.

Companion videos and activity guides, as well as multimedia kits for classroom use, are also available. MarshMedia has been publishing high-quality, award-winning learning materials for children since 1969. To order or to receive a free catalog, call 1-800-821-3303, or visit us at www.marshmedia.com.

## NEW SPAIN

In 1519, Hernán Cortés arrived on the shores of America. He and his Spanish conquistadors quickly defeated the last of Mexico's great Indian empires — the Aztec. Spanish officials followed the conquistadors and established a colony called New Spain. During the next 300 years, Spanish culture became part of Mexico's heritage. The colonists brought the Spanish language — the official language of Mexico today — and the Roman Catholic religion. They built homes and cities in the Spanish style. They introduced citrus fruits, cheese, and wheat to the Mexican diet. They brought livestock — horses and oxen, mules and burros — to carry heavy burdens. Mexicans mastered the skills of the charro riders and wore their Spanish costumes. They learned the art of bullfighting — invented in Spain — and built the world's largest bullring in Mexico City. The Spanish brought to Mexico their love of literature and many of their arts and crafts, such the making of beautiful ceramic tiles and colorful *piñatas*.

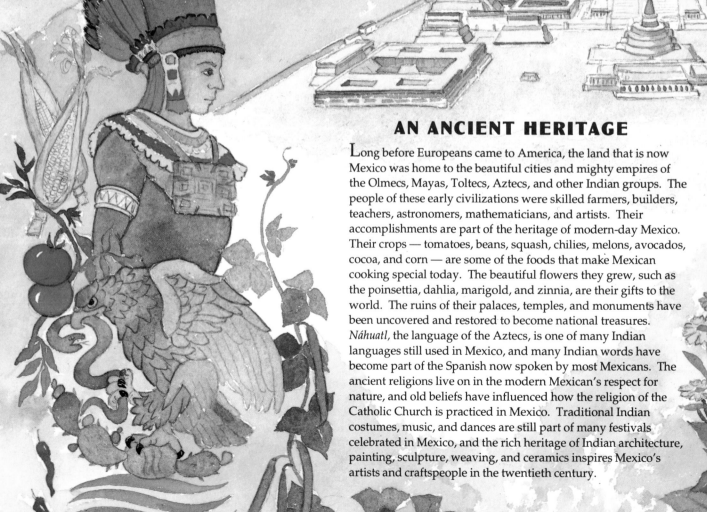

## AN ANCIENT HERITAGE

Long before Europeans came to America, the land that is now Mexico was home to the beautiful cities and mighty empires of the Olmecs, Mayas, Toltecs, Aztecs, and other Indian groups. The people of these early civilizations were skilled farmers, builders, teachers, astronomers, mathematicians, and artists. Their accomplishments are part of the heritage of modern-day Mexico. Their crops — tomatoes, beans, squash, chilies, melons, avocados, cocoa, and corn — are some of the foods that make Mexican cooking special today. The beautiful flowers they grew, such as the poinsettia, dahlia, marigold, and zinnia, are their gifts to the world. The ruins of their palaces, temples, and monuments have been uncovered and restored to become national treasures. *Náhuatl*, the language of the Aztecs, is one of many Indian languages still used in Mexico, and many Indian words have become part of the Spanish now spoken by most Mexicans. The ancient religions live on in the modern Mexican's respect for nature, and old beliefs have influenced how the religion of the Catholic Church is practiced in Mexico. Traditional Indian costumes, music, and dances are still part of many festivals celebrated in Mexico, and the rich heritage of Indian architecture, painting, sculpture, weaving, and ceramics inspires Mexico's artists and craftspeople in the twentieth century.